LUCY
TRIES
SHORT TRACK

written by

Lisa Bowes

illustrated by

James Hearne

ORCA BOOK PUBLISHERS

Ava and Claire,

Rachel and Jill,

RACHEL

JILL

together
they practice
to learn this
new skill.

They're trying speed skating, so they skate really fast and always to the left.

It's called short track!

They each wear a helmet and skin suits to match with lots of protection in case there's a crash.

They go to the line...
It's time for the race!

Lucy's on the **inside**
(that's the **very best** place).

BANG! goes the start gun.
They're around the
first turn.

Lucy **charges** ahead,
her blades ready to **burn.**

'Round, 'round they go—
good **balance** is key.

Look how close they are!
That's a **pack**,
you see.

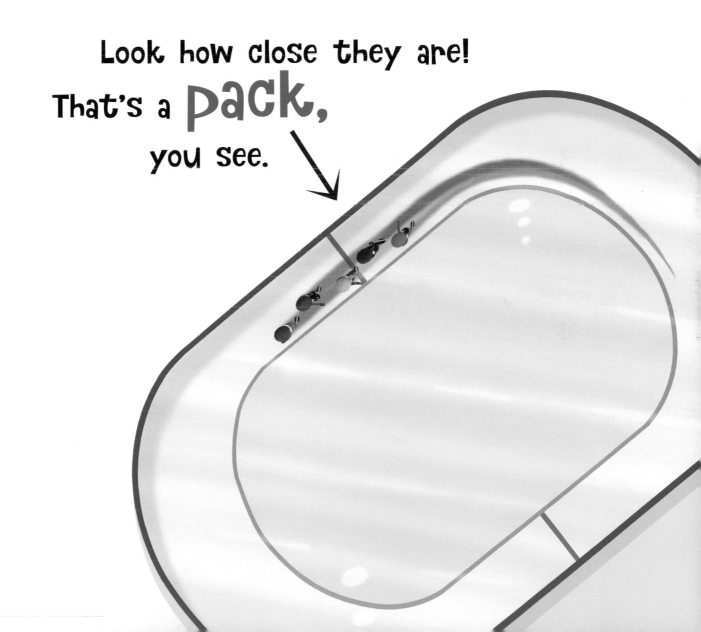

They **lean** into each corner,
hands touching the ice,
on pace for a **record**—
now **that** would be nice!

What a fight for the lead!

They're going **So fast...**

but just then Claire slips—

she's going to **Crash!**

Claire hits the safety pads.

BOOM!

She's out of the race.

"It's all right. I'm okay."

It just means

fifth place.

Claire cheers on the rest.
Now Lucy leads the pack.
Can she stay in first?
There's the bell.

It's last lap!

She feels someone close—
it's Jill **right behind.**

One last tight curve...

Quick!
There's
the line!

They're neck and neck,
two skaters, two friends.

Here's the **final stride**...
Jill wins in the end!

"Way to go!" Lucy says
with a hug for Claire too.
"Great race, Jill!" she adds.

"I'm so happy for you!"

It's fun to skate fast
with old friends and new.

Will **you** try **short track?**
It's a **cool sport** to do!

FAST FACTS!

THE BLADE—The blade is the part of the skate that touches the ice. Speed skates have longer blades than hockey or figure skates do because a longer blade helps a skater go faster!

THE SKIN SUIT—The inside of this special suit is lined with "cut-proof" material to keep the skater safe from the blades.

THE RINK—A short-track race takes place on a small oval ice surface similar to the size of a hockey rink. Because the skaters are almost always skating around a curve, the tight corners make it challenging for them to stay in control.

HOW OLD IS SHORT-TRACK SPEED SKATING?
Short track is over a hundred years old! It originated in North America in 1905.

THE SAFETY PADS—The vinyl-covered, foam-filled crash pads help to cushion skaters' bodies when they fall. The pads were once set up against the rink's boards. Now there's a "boardless" system designed by Canadian scientists and engineers that makes short track much safer for the skaters.

For my brother Daniel
—L.B.

For my three girls, Paula, Mikayla and Vicky
—J.H.

Text copyright © 2016 Lisa Bowes
Illustrations copyright © 2016 James Hearne

Library and Archives Canada Cataloguing in Publication

Bowes, Lisa, 1966–, author
Lucy tries short track / Lisa Bowes ; illustrated by James Hearne.
(Lucy tries sports)

Originally published: [Calgary, Alberta] : Bowes Knows Sports, 2014.

Issued in print and electronic formats.
ISBN 978-1-4598-1025-9 (paperback).—ISBN 978-1-4598-1026-6 (pdf).—
ISBN 978-1-4598-1027-3 (epub)

I. Hearne, James, 1972–, illustrator II. Title.
PS8603.O9758L837 2016   jC813'.6   C2015-904470-7
C2015-904471-5

First published in the United States, 2016
Library of Congress Control Number: 2015947568

Summary: In this picture book and follow-up to *Lucy Tries Luge*, Lucy and her friends lace up their skates and try short track speed skating.

MIX
Paper from responsible sources
FSC
www.fsc.org
FSC® C016245

Orca Book Publishers is dedicated to preserving the environment and has printed this book on Forest Stewardship Council® certified paper.

Orca Book Publishers gratefully acknowledges the support for its publishing programs provided by the following agencies: the Government of Canada through the Canada Book Fund and the Canada Council for the Arts, and the Province of British Columbia through the BC Arts Council and the Book Publishing Tax Credit.

Artwork created using hand drawings and digital coloring.

Cover artwork by James Hearne
Design by Teresa Bubela

ORCA BOOK PUBLISHERS
www.orcabook.com

Printed and bound in Canada.

19 18 17 16 • 4 3 2 1